Celebrate reading with us!

Cover and title page illustrations by John Sandford.

Acknowledgments appear on page 158.

1995 Impression
Copyright © 1993 by Houghton Mifflin Company. All rights reserved.

Printed in the U.S.A.

ISBN: 0-395-61080-X

6789-D-96 95

DREAM A STORY

Senior Author
John J. Pikulski

Senior Coordinating Author
J. David Cooper

Senior Consulting Author
William K. Durr

Coordinating Authors
Kathryn H. Au
M. Jean Greenlaw
Marjorie Y. Lipson
Susan E. Page
Sheila W. Valencia
Karen K. Wixson

Authors
Rosalinda B. Barrera
Edwina Bradley
Ruth P. Bunyan
Jacqueline L. Chaparro
Jacqueline C. Comas
Alan N. Crawford
Robert L. Hillerich
Timothy G. Johnson
Jana M. Mason
Pamela A. Mason
William E. Nagy
Joseph S. Renzulli
Alfredo Schifini

Senior Advisor
Richard C. Anderson

Advisors
Christopher J. Baker
Charles Peters
MaryEllen Vogt

HOUGHTON MIFFLIN COMPANY   BOSTON

Atlanta   Dallas   Geneva, Illinois   Palo Alto   Princeton   Toronto

3

🏵 Award Winner

THEME 2

8

WILD ANIMALS, COME OUT!

If you met a wild animal, it just might hide from you! Where do you think it might go? The animals in these stories have some funny hiding places. Read about these animals and join them in a game of hide-and-seek.

Big Book

Monkeys in the Jungle
Angie Sage

The animals in this book live in many different places. They also like to hide! Can you guess where they are?

Read this book together to find out where the animals might be.

CONTENTS

TO DESERT

by Pat Mora

illustrated by Diana McKnight

Listen to the desert,
Pon, pon, pon.

Listen to the desert,
Pon, pon, pon.

Listen to the owl say,
"Whoo, whoo, whoo."

Listen to the owl say,
"Whoo, whoo, whoo."

Listen to the toad hop,
Plop, plop, plop.

Listen to the toad hop,
Plop, plop, plop.

Listen to the snake say,
"Tst-tst-tst."

Listen to the snake say,
"Tst-tst-tst."

Listen to the dove say,
"Coo, coo, coo."

Listen to the dove say,
"Coo, coo, coo."

Listen to the coyote say,
"Aroo, aroo, aroo."

Listen to the coyote say,
"Aroo, aroo, aroo."

Listen to the fish jump,
Plunk, plunk, plunk.

Listen to the fish jump,
Plunk, plunk, plunk.

Listen to the mice run,
Scrit, scrit, scrit.

Listen to the mice run,
Scrit, scrit, scrit.

Listen to the rain dance,
Plip, plip, plip.

Listen to the rain dance,
Plip, plip, plip.

Listen to the wind sing,
Swish, swish, swish.

Listen to the wind sing,
Swish, swish, swish.

Listen to the desert,
Pon, pon, pon.

Listen to the desert,
Pon, pon, pon.

Add New Animal Sounds

The mouse in this poem made a *scrit* sound when it ran.

Think of some other desert animals and the sounds they might make. Make a list. Then write a new verse for the poem.

Meet the Author Pat Mora grew up in El Paso, Texas, near the Mexican border. Much of her poetry is about life in the southwestern United States, which Pat Mora calls "my world."

Besides writing, Ms. Mora likes to read, dance, and spend time with friends. She lives in Cincinnati, Ohio.

Meet the Illustrator Diana McKnight is a graphic designer, which means she arranges the pictures and words for books and book covers. She has been drawing since she was a little girl. As an adult, Ms. McKnight still loves to draw pictures — especially pictures of animals.

I Caught a Fish

illustrated by R.W. Alley

One, two, three, four, five,
Once I caught a fish alive,

Six, seven, eight, nine, ten,
Then I let it go again.

One, two, three, four, five,
Once I caught a bird alive,

Six, seven, eight, nine, ten,
Then I let it go again.

One, two, three, four, five,
Once I caught a giraffe alive,

Six, seven, eight, nine, ten,
Then I let it go again.

One, two, three, four, five,
Once I caught a LION alive,

Six, seven, eight, nine, ten,
Then I let it go again!

FROGGIE, FROGGIE

Froggie, froggie.
Hoppity-hop!
When you get to the sea
You do not stop.

Plop!

閙來無事叫嘎嘎不叫爸爸叫媽媽

河蟆河蟆跳搭搭搭東洋大海有他家

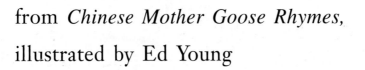

from *Chinese Mother Goose Rhymes,*
illustrated by Ed Young

Lion

Look!
A lion!
Mighty beast.
   (Might he
   Bite me
   For a feast?)
Though I know
He wouldn't dare,
   I'm mighty glad

he's over there.

by Mary Ann Hoberman

36

SOPHIE & JACK

by *Judy Taylor*

illustrated by Susan Gantner

It was a wonderful day for a picnic.

Everyone was hungry.

Soon there was not much left.

"Let's play hide-and-seek," said Sophie.

"I'll hide," said Jack.

"I'll seek," said Sophie.

Jack hid behind a tree with his eyes shut tight.

Sophie shut her eyes, too, and counted to ten.

Sophie found Jack very quickly.

"Now me," she said.

Jack turned his back and counted to ten.

Sophie hid in the grass with her eyes
shut tight.

Jack found her very quickly.

"Me again," said Jack, and he ran off
to hide.

Sophie couldn't find Jack anywhere.

Can you?

Where's Sophie?

It's Sophie's turn to hide again. Can you think of a good hiding place for her — a place where Jack won't find her?

Draw a picture of Sophie's new hiding place and write a sentence about it.

Meet the Author
Judy Taylor

Judy Taylor used to help other authors write books. She did such a good job that the Queen of England gave her a prize!

Now Mrs. Taylor writes her own books. She began with *Sophie and Jack*. Later on, she also wrote some storybooks about a mouse named Dudley.

Meet the Illustrator
Susan Gantner

Susan Gantner's drawings can be seen in museums. She first drew pictures of hippos for greeting cards. Then she began to draw pictures for Judy Taylor's books. After that, her two hippos became known as Sophie and Jack.

One Little Elephant

from a traditional counting rhyme in English

One little elephant,
Out for a run,
Climbed up a spider's web
Just for fun.
He tiptoed across,
He did a little dance,
And then he called down
For some *more* ele–phants.

Two little elephants,
Out for a run ...

Three little elephants ...

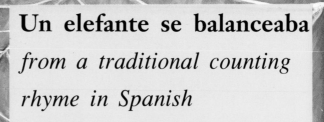

Un elefante se balanceaba

from a traditional counting rhyme in Spanish

Un elefante
se balanceaba
sobre la tela
de una araña,
como veía
que resistía
fue a llamar
a otro elefante.

Dos elefantes
se balanceaban . . .

Tres elefantes . . .

HAVE YOU SEEN THE CROCODILE?

Written and Illustrated by Colin West

"Have you seen the crocodile?" asked the parrot.

"No,"
said the
dragonfly.

"Have you seen the crocodile?"
asked the parrot
and the dragonfly.

"No,"
said the
bumble bee.

"Have you seen the crocodile?"
asked the parrot
and the dragonfly
and the bumble bee.

"No,"
said the
butterfly.

"Have you seen the crocodile?"
asked the parrot
and the dragonfly
and the bumble bee
and the butterfly.

"No,"
said the
hummingbird.

"Have you seen the crocodile?"
asked the parrot
and the dragonfly
and the bumble bee
and the butterfly
and the hummingbird.

"No," said the frog.

"No one's seen the crocodile!"
said the parrot
and the dragonfly
and the bumble bee
and the butterfly
and the hummingbird
and the frog.

"I'VE SEEN THE CROCODILE!" snapped the crocodile.

"But, has anyone seen the parrot
and the dragonfly
and the bumble bee
and the butterfly
and the hummingbird
and the frog?"

asked the crocodile.

Jungle Puppets

When the crocodile said, "I'VE SEEN THE CROCODILE," how do you think it sounded?

Make some puppets like the animals in the story. Then as you read the story aloud, put on a jungle puppet play! Make your animals sound just like the ones in the story.

Meet the Author and Illustrator
Colin West

When he was a little boy, Colin West practiced magic tricks. He also liked to read about plants and animals.

When he grew up, Mr. West went to art school. He has been writing and drawing pictures for storybooks ever since. He also writes poetry.

MORE WILD ANIMALS

Monkeys in the Jungle
by Angie Sage

You know where the monkeys live. Now read the book again. Can you remember where all the other animals live?

Read Alone Books

Let's Jump!
Who Will Read to Me?
Come Out, Bear!

I Am Eyes
Ni Macho

by Leila Ward

An African boy wakes up to see giraffes and flamingos. Find out about the other wild animals he meets in this book.

We Hide, You Seek

*by Jose Aruego
and Ariane Dewey*

A rhinoceros wants to play hide-and-seek with its friends. Read about all the good hiding places they find!

"Pardon?" Said the Giraffe

by Colin West

A frog wonders what it's like to be tall, like Giraffe. Then Frog takes a ride on Giraffe's nose — and gets a surprise!

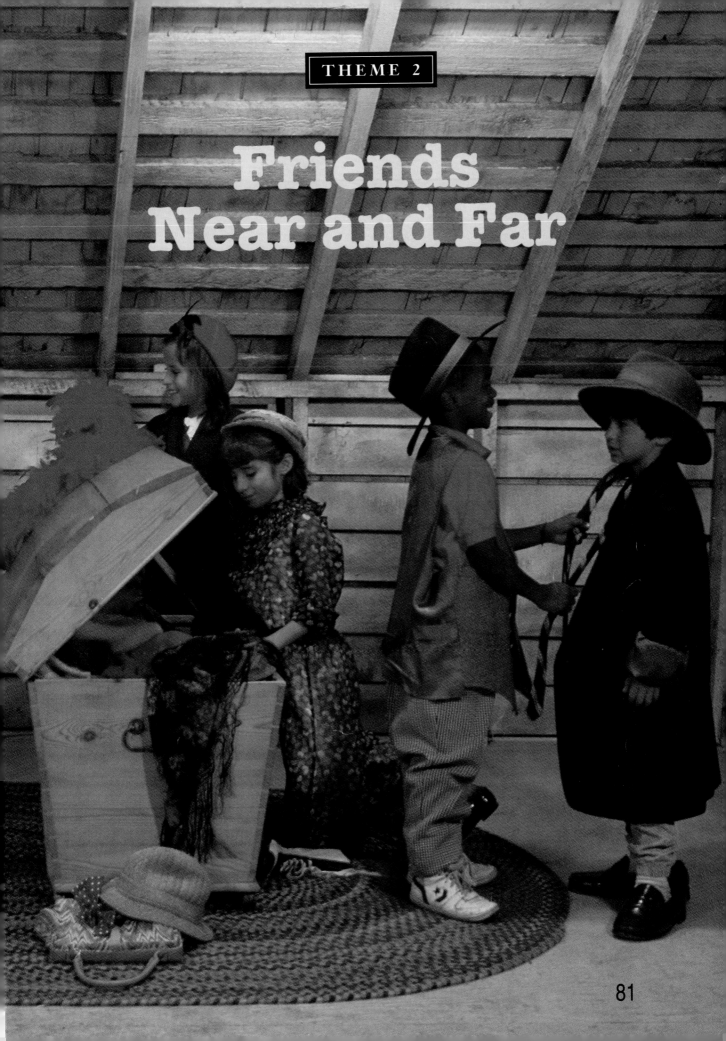

Friends Near and Far

What is more fun than doing something you like? Doing something you like with a friend! Read these stories and poems about friends close to home and friends from far away. Then read them with one of *your* friends, and share some good times.

Contents

A PLAYHOUSE FOR MONSTER

by Virginia Mueller

illustrated by Lynn Munsinger

Monster made a sign. It said KEEP OUT!

"This is *my* playhouse," Monster said.

"These are *my* walls."

"*My* roof."

"*My* windows."

"*My* door."

"*My* chair."

"*My* table."

"*My* cookie."

"*My* glass of milk."

But Monster wasn't happy.

"I know," he said.
"I need *two* chairs."

"*Two* cookies."

"*Two* glasses of milk."

Monster made a new sign.
It said WELCOME!

Make Posters, Make Friends!

Monster made a new sign for the playhouse. It said "Welcome." Can you think of some good ways to make a friend feel welcome?

Make a poster about one of your ideas. You could roll up your poster and put a ribbon around it. Then you could give it to a special friend!

Meet the Author

When Virginia Mueller was a little girl, she liked to read poetry. Her first poem was published when she was only ten years old! Since then, Mrs. Mueller has written more than fifteen storybooks.

Meet the Illustrator

Lynn Munsinger draws many kinds of pictures, but most of all she likes to draw monsters. She doesn't like scary ones. She likes to draw the funny kind — like Monster and his friend!

You'll Sing a Song and I'll Sing a Song

a song by Ella Jenkins

You'll sing a song
And I'll sing a song
Then we'll sing a song together

You'll sing a song
And I'll sing a song
In warm or wintry weather

You'll play a tune
And I'll play a tune
Then we'll play a tune together

You'll play a tune
And I'll play a tune
In warm or wintry weather

You'll hum a line
And I'll hum a line
Then we'll hum a line together

You'll hum a line
And I'll hum a line
In warm or wintry weather

You'll whistle a while
And I'll whistle a while
Then we'll whistle a while together

You'll whistle a while
And I'll whistle a while
In warm or wintry weather

SCHOOL DAYS

By B.G. Hennessy

Pictures by Tracey Campbell Pearson

School bus, cubby, starting bell

Circle time, then show and tell.

Bookshelves, desks, pencil sharpener,

New friends, old friends, plant monitor.

Shapes and numbers, alphabet,
Puzzles, blocks, classroom pet.

Making rhymes and letter games,
Telling time and learning names.

Matthew, Dee, Mark and Claire,
Jason, Nancy and Pierre.

Molly, Sam and Gregory,
Ruby, Max and Hillary.

Daniel, Jill and Jennifer,
Gail, Rebecca, Christopher.

Crayons, scissors, markers, glue,

Smocks and paper, a perfect blue.

Music teacher, Librarian,

Coach and Nurse, Custodian.

Lunch box, sandwich, popcorn, juice,

Cookies, apple, Matt's front tooth!

Recess, fun time, run, jump, race,
Ball and tag, touch home base.

Feeling sad, feeling mad,
Someone has been very bad.

Seesaw, swings and sky high slides,

One more minute, one last ride.

Hearing stories, sitting still,

Listen, line up, fire drill!

Writing, reading, practicing,
Waiting for the bell to ring.

Backpack, work book, pencil case,
Everything is in its place.

Now it's time for school to end
Say goodbye to all your friends.

Write to a Friend

What part of the school day
do you like best?
Write a letter to a friend.
In your letter, tell about something
fun you did at school. You might
try making some of your lines rhyme,
as the ones in the story do.

Meet the Author

B. G. Hennessy's job is to direct people who draw pictures for books. She worked with Tracey Campbell Pearson on another book called *The Missing Tarts*, which won a prize. Ms. Hennessy lives in New York with her husband and two sons.

Meet the Illustrator

After Tracey Campbell Pearson went to art school, she began illustrating children's books. Some of them are about characters named Claude and Shirley, and are written by Joan L. Nixon. Tracey Campbell Pearson's drawings have also appeared on cards and in magazines. She lives in Vermont.

from *Something on My Mind*

Waiting
for lunchtime.
When it comes,
the school day will be
half over
and we can go
play doubledutch.

by Nikki Grimes

Poems About Friends

The New Girl

I can feel
we're much the same,
though I don't
know your name.

What friends
we're going to be
when I know you
and you know me!

by Charlotte Zolotow

J A M B O

Jambo		Jambo
ambo		ambo
mbo		mbo
bo	bo	bo
o	o	o
bo	bo	bo
mbo		mbo
ambo		ambo
Jambo		Jambo
HI!		HELLO!
Did you		Did you
did you		know
Jambo		means
hello		hello!

by Sundaira Morninghouse

Friends Around the World

MEXICO

SPAIN

RUSSIA

KENYA

CHINA

CANADA

CZECHOSLOVAKIA

ECUADOR

BHUTAN

Dear Friends,

My name is Angela and I live in Kotzebue, Alaska. My people are called Inupiat, which means "the real people" in our language.

Where I live, it is light for twenty-four hours a day in the summer. If we wanted to, we could ride our bikes at midnight because it is still daylight outside! In winter, it is dark twenty-four hours a day. We spend a lot of time indoors then.

We have learned ways to live in the cold weather here. And we love the special beauty of our homeland. I can't imagine living anywhere else!

Angela

138

The ice is breaking up!
My family and I know
summer is beginning.

My mother mends the
cloth cover for the fur
parky I will wear this
season.

I watch Vera add floats
to the fish net.

My friend and I help wash
and clean the fish, which will
be hung on a rack to dry.

139

Time to have fun! This game is called the nalukataq, or blanket toss.

On special days we celebrate with dances and songs. The elders play flat drums called gilaun.

My family and I love pizza! My mother cuts it with an ulu.

My friend and I run in a three-legged race.

TOBY IN THE COUNTRY,

TOBY IN THE CITY

by Maxine Zohn Bozzo • illustrated by Frank Modell

I live in the country, and my name is Toby.

I live in the city, and my name is Toby.

My house looks like this.

My house looks like this.

My street looks like this, and has trees.

My street looks like this, and has trees.

I go to school with my sister and brother.

I go to school with my sister and brother.

After school I like to play with my friends.

After school I like to play with my friends.

Sometimes it's winter in the country . . .
and I like to play in the snow.

Sometimes it's winter in the city . . .
and I like to play in the snow.

When it is spring in the country . . .
I see lots of flowers.

When it is spring in the city . . .
I see lots of flowers.

When summer comes to the country . . .
I like to go to the beach.

When summer comes to the city . . .
I like to go to the beach.

Sometimes when it is fall in the country . . .
I like to play in the leaves.

Sometimes when it is fall in the city . . .
I like to play in the leaves.

I like to live in the country.

I like to live in the city.

I like to visit the city.

I like to visit the country.

And I LIKE YOU!

A BOOK ABOUT YOU

You have learned some things about the country Toby and the city Toby. Now make a book about *you*. Tell about yourself and where you live. Then let your friends read all about you.

Meet the Author

Maxine Bozzo grew up in New York City. She spends most of her time writing. Ms. Bozzo also helps artists sell their work, and she makes jewelry out of beads. Ms. Bozzo is married to an artist. They have three children.

Meet the Illustrator

Frank Modell was drawing cartoons before he was in kindergarten! When he grew up, Mr. Modell wrote and illustrated storybooks and did some art work for the *Sesame Street* and *The Electric Company* TV shows.

Today Mr. Modell draws cartoons for a magazine.

Drawing by Modell, (c) 1983
The New Yorker Magazine, Inc.

Read Alone Books

Meet More Friends

I Need a Friend *by Sherry Kafka*

Together you read about the two new friends in this book. Now read it again — to one of *your* friends!

A Country Far Away *by Nigel Gray*

Do you like to read about places far away? Then you'll love this book about two boys from different countries. You'll be surprised at how alike they are!

I Have a Friend *by Keiko Narahashi*

A boy tells about a special friend who follows him everywhere. You have a friend like this, too!

The Friend *by John Burningham*

A boy and his best friend argue over a toy. Will they ever be friends again?

Acknowledgments

For each of the selections listed below, grateful acknowledgment is made for permission to excerpt and/or reprint original or copyrighted material, as follows:

Major Selections

Have You Seen the Crocodile? by Colin West (J. B. Lippincott). Copyright © 1986 by Colin West. Reprinted by permission of Harper and Row, Publishers, Inc.

"Listen to the Desert" by Pat Mora. Used by permission of the author.

A Playhouse for Monster, text copyright © 1985 by Virginia Mueller. Illustrations copyright © 1985 by Lynn Munsinger. Originally published in hardcover by Albert Whitman and Company. All rights reserved. Used with permission.

From *School Days* by B.G. Hennessy, illustrated by Tracey Campbell Pearson. Text copyright © 1990 by B.G. Hennessy. Illustrations copyright © 1990 by Tracey Campbell Pearson. Used by permission of Viking Penguin, a division of Penguin Books USA Inc.

Sophie and Jack, text copyright © 1982 by Judy Taylor, illustrations copyright © 1982 by Susan Gantner. Reprinted by permission of Philomel Books, and The Bodley Head.

Toby in the Country, Toby in the City by Maxine Zohn Bozzo, illustrated by Frank Modell. Text copyright © 1982 by Maxine Zohn Bozzo. Illustrations copyright © 1982 by Frank Modell. Reprinted by permission of Greenwillow Books, a division of William Morrow and Co., Inc.

"You'll Sing a Song and I'll Sing a Song" from *The Ella Jenkins Song Book For Children* by Ella Jenkins. Copyright © 1966 Oak Publications. Reprinted by permission of Ell-Bern Publishing Company (A. S. C. A. P.).

Poetry

"Froggie, Froggie" from *Chinese Mother Goose Rhymes*, selected and edited by Robert Wyndham, pictures by Ed Young. Copyright © 1968 by Robert Wyndham. Illustrations copyright © 1968 by Ed Young. Reprinted by permission of Philomel Books.

"Jambo" from *Nightfeathers* by Sundaira Morninghouse. Copyright © 1989 by Sundaira Morninghouse. Reprinted by permission of Open Hand Publishing Inc.

"Lion" from *The Raucous Auk* by Mary Ann Hoberman. Text copyright © 1973 by Mary Ann Hoberman. Reprinted by permission of the Gina Maccoby Literary Agency.

"The New Girl" from *Everything Glistens and Everything Sings* by Charlotte Zolotow. Copyright © 1987 by Charlotte Zolotow. Reprinted by permission of Harcourt Brace Jovanovich, Inc.

"Waiting for Lunchtime" from *Something On My Mind* by Nikki Grimes. Copyright © 1978 by Nikki Grimes. Reprinted by permission of Penguin USA and Nikki Grimes.

Others

Cartoon by Frank Modell from *The New Yorker Cartoon Album 1975-1985*. Copyright © 1975-1985. Reprinted by permission.

Credits

Program Design   Carbone Smolan Associates

Cover Design   Carbone Smolan Associates

Design   8–79 Sibley/Peteet Design, Inc.;   80–157 Michael P. Cronan Design

Introduction   (left to right) 1st row: John Sandford; Diana McKnight; R. W. Alley;   2nd row: R. W. Alley; John Lei; Diana McKnight;   3rd row: Frank Siteman; Catharine O'Neill; Diane Jaquith;   4th row: R. W. Alley; Diana McKnight; S. Ogilvy

Table of Contents   4 John Sandford;   6 Ellen Joy Sasaki

Illustration   8–11 John Sandford;   12–27 Diana McKnight; 28–33 R. W. Alley;   34 Ed Young;   35 Diana McKnight; 36–55 Susan Gantner;   56–57 Diane Jaquith;   58–75 Colin West;   76 Chris Froeter;   77 Colin West;   78–79 John Sandford;   84–99 Lynn Munsinger;   101 Susan Jaekel; 102–105 Ellen Joy Sasaki;   106–130 Tracey Campbell Pearson;   131 David Diaz;   132 Susan Jaekel;   133 David Murray;   134 Catharine O'Neill;   135 Peg McGovern; 141–153 Frank Modell;   154 Catharine O'Neill;   155 Susan Jaekel

Photography   27 Courtesy of Pat Mora (top);   27 Steve Woods (bottom);   100 Alec Duncan (bottom);   101 Nancy Pieper/The Sheboygan Press (top);   101 Courtesy of Lynn Munsinger (bottom);   132 Courtesy of Tracey Campbell Pearson (bottom);   132 Courtesy of B.G. Hennessy (top); 136 Bob Daemmrich (top);   136 © David Ball/The Stock Market (center left);   136 Bruce Davidson/Magnum (center right);   136 Paul Conklin/Uniphoto (bottom); 137 Eastcott/Momatiuk/Woodfin Camp and Associates (center left);   137 Karen Rantzman (center right);   137 P. & G. Bowater/The Image Bank (top left);   137 David Falconer/Frazier Library (top right);   137 © Susan Katz (bottom);   138–140 Lawrence Migdale;   155 Courtesy of

Maxine Bozzo (top);   **155** Anne Hall (bottom)

Assignment Photographers   Brent Jones   **131**; Elliott
Smith   **80–81, 82–83, 156–157** (2-page spread)